THE STORY OF
HENNY PENNY

Illustrated by *Tom and Blonnie Holmes*

HENNY-PENNY

COCKY-LOCKY

GOOSEY-LOOSEY

FOXY-WOXY

TURKEY-LURKEY

THE CASTLE

DUCKY-DADDLES

THE KING

IT'S FUN TO READ ALONG

Here's what you do—

These pictures are some of the characters and things the story tells about. Let the child to whom you are reading SEE and SAY them.

Then, as you read the story text and come to a picture instead of a word, pause and point to the picture for your listener to SEE and SAY.

You'll be amazed at how quickly children catch on and enjoy participating in the story-telling.

IBSN-10: 0-86163-808-5
ISBN-13: 978-0-86163-808-6
Copyright © 1984 Award Publications Limited
This edition first published 1995
Seventh impression 2007
Published by Award Publications Limited, The Old Riding School,
The Welbeck Estate, Worksop, Nottinghamshire, S80 3LR
Printed in Malaysia

HENNY PENNY

One day  was picking up

 in the yard when—

whack! Something fell and

hit her on the

"Oh, dear me!" said

"The sky is falling. I must

go and tell the  ."

Off she went down the

and met  who said,

"Good morning, . Where are

you going this fine day?"

"I'm going to tell the  that

the  is falling," said  .

"A piece of it fell on my ."

"May I go, too?" asked  .

 answered, "Come along."

They set off to find the  .

They went past  and

past  and soon they

met 🦆 waddling down

the dusty ⌒ .

"Good morning,  and

 ," said  . "Where

are you going this fine day?"

"We're going to tell the

that the is falling," said

 . "A piece of it fell on

the top of my  ."

"May I go, too?"  asked.

"Come along," said  ,

and they all set off together to

find the of the 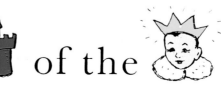 .

They passed a  on a

and a  with a and

soon they met  hurrying

along down the dusty 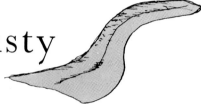 .

"Good morning, friends.

Where are you going this

fine day?" asked  .

"We're going to tell the

that the is falling," said .

"A piece of it fell on my ."

"May I go with you?" asked .

"Come along," said  ,

and they set off together to

find the of the  .

They went through a  and

behind a and soon they

met coming along down

the long dusty .

"Good morning. Where are

you going?" asked

"We're going to tell the

the ▨ is falling," said  .

"A piece of it fell on my ,"

 asked, "May I go too?"

 said, "Come along," and

they all went off to find the

of the  . They crossed a

 and went over

and soon met  coming

down the  .

"Good morning," said  .

"Where are you going this fine

day?" answered, "We're

on our way to tell the

that the  is falling. A

piece of it fell on my ."

"May I go, too?" asked .

 said, "Come along,"

and they all set off together

to find the of the  .

Suddenly stopped in

the middle of the  and

said, "Oh, dear me, this isn't

the way to the of

the 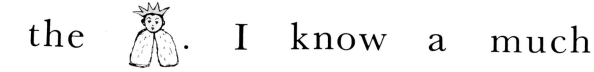. I know a much

shorter 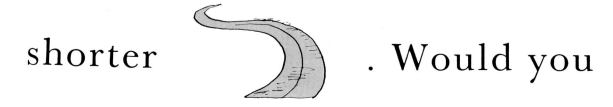. Would you

like me to show it to you?"

"That would be very kind of

you ," said  ,  ,

 ,  , and  .

They all went along together

to tell the  that the  was

falling. They went past

and more , and finally

they came to a dark

where 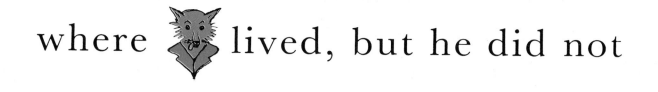 lived, but he did not

tell them so.  said, "Here

is the short cut to the

. We'll get there soon if

you follow me. I'll go first, and

you come after me, one at a

time— ,  ,  ,

 , and ."

Then led the way

into his , and waited for

them to come in after him.

And they did follow him, just

as he had told them.

went in first, and he had not

gone very far before

snapped off his .

   went in next, and she

had not gone very far before

 snapped off her .

 was next. He had not

gone very far either before

snapped off his

Then  went in. As soon

as he saw , he called out to

 very loudly, and she ran

home as fast as she could.

And so  never got to

tell the  that the

was falling, after all.